S0-BZR-377

*S*hooting *S*tardust

By Frrich Lewandowski

Illustrations by Kathryn H. Delisle

Ambassador Books
Worcester, Massachusetts

Shooting Stardust

Copyright 1998 by Richard P. Lewandowski
All rights reserved. No part of this book may be reproduced or transmitted in any form or by any means, electronic or mechanical, including photocopying, recording, or by any information or retrieval system, without written permission from the Publisher.

Library of Congress Catalog Card Number 98-92523

Printed in Singapore

ISBN: 0-9646439-4-4

Published by: Ambassador Books, Inc.
                71 Elm Street
                Worcester, MA 01609

To order, call: 800 577-0909

Shooting Stardust
is dedicated to my sister,
Carolyn Elizabeth Lewandowski Killelea,
whose premature passing
was the catalyst for its penning.

It is also dedicated to
all those whose lives ended too soon.

If, as a result of reading *Shooting Stardust*,
anyone might find it cathartic to share their story
regarding the loss of a child or sibling,
please write to me at
25 Darnell Road, Worcester, MA 01606

Frrich Lewandowski

Every year, Kyle, Joey, and their Mom and Dad went to the beach for their summer vacation. They all loved the beach for their own special reasons.

Dad enjoyed going out on a big boat and fishing.

Mom liked to order lobster whenever the family went out to dinner at a restaurant.

Kyle preferred to swim in the ocean and body-surf the waves to shore.

Joey liked to walk by the beach, look for shells, and build sand castles.

Vacations by the sea were great because there was no T.V. in
their summer home. Every evening after dinner, the family would play games, or take long walks together.

Joey and Kyle would walk ahead of their parents along the
dark path. Every time the boys would see a shooting star, they
would ask their parents, "Did you see the shooting star?" Most
of the time, their parents would respond by saying, "no". Once,
Joey asked his older brother why Mom and Dad didn't see the
shooting stars. Kyle explained to his little brother that when
people get older, sometimes their eyes don't work so well and
so they don't always see what children see.

6

Joey asked his brother what shooting stars were. Kyle said he really didn't know for sure, but had heard that they were angels who brought special messages from heaven to people on earth who needed to hear that special message. Joey said that he hoped one day he'd get his own special message from heaven. "Maybe one day you will," Kyle said, "maybe one day you will."

That year, after their vacation, Kyle got sick and wasn't get-ting any better. Mom took him to see the doctor. The doctor said that Kyle would have to go to the hospital for a few days for some tests. Joey missed his brother very much but visited him every day.

Kyle came home but never got better. In fact, he seemed to get worse day after day. He went back and forth to the hospital many times and then, finally, didn't return. His Mom and Dad came home from the hospital one day and were very sad. They told Joey that Kyle wouldn't be coming home again. They said that Kyle had died. Joey felt bad. He already missed his brother. He could see that his Mom and Dad would miss Kyle too.

The year after Kyle died, holidays just weren't the same.

Halloween was always fun when Joey and Kyle would dress up and go trick-or-treating together. But this year, Joey went trick-or-treating with a friend. Though it was okay, it sure seemed different and definitely less fun than it was before with Kyle.

On Thanksgiving Day, the family went to Grandma and Grandpa's house as they always had in the past. Since Kyle died, however, everyone was so sad, and they kept talking about him.

Joey especially missed his brother on Christmas morning.
Every year, the two boys would wake each other up to see
what Santa brought. They had such fun seeing what each had
received and playing with all their toys and games. This year
was so sad. . . waking up and checking out the presents *alone*,
that Joey believed that it didn't even feel like Christmas!

Easter had always been so special. In past years, Mom always bought the boys new suits to wear for Church. Both Kyle and Joey liked to dress up in their new Easter outfits and wear them for all of Easter Sunday. This year, everything was different. In fact, things had changed so much since Kyle died, that Mom even forgot to buy Joey a new suit.

It was coming time for summer vacation at the beach. Mom and Dad wondered if the family should go. Maybe they should just stay home, Mom thought. Joey knew that Mom didn't want to go because she still missed Kyle. In the end, they decided to go.

When they arrived at the cottage, Mom began to cry. Dad tried to make her feel better. He took her out for lobster that evening. Joey kept doing things to try to make Mom and Dad laugh. . . things that he and Kyle would do that had made them laugh before. Now, however, it seemed that nothing could be done to make them laugh and be happy.

That first night on vacation, Joey couldn't sleep. He missed his brother so much. He knew that the reason Mom and Dad were so sad was that they missed Kyle too. He stared out the window and gazed at the stars. Suddenly, he saw a shooting star, bigger and brighter than any shooting star that he and Kyle had ever seen before!

Joey kept watching as the star got bigger and bigger . . . closer and closer until the light came and landed right on the porch by Joey's bedroom window! He thought, at first, that he was dreaming. When he realized he wasn't, he got out of bed and rushed toward the window.

There, on the porch, was Kyle. Joey was so excited! He went to get Mom and Dad, but Kyle called him back.

"Don't wake Mom and Dad," Kyle said.
Joey responded, "Why not? They'll be so happy to see you."

"They won't see me, Joey," Kyle explained, "because when people get older, their eyes don't work so well and so they don't always see what children see. In the morning, just tell them that I came by to let them know that they don't have to be sad because I'm all right and very happy. Tell them that I'll even be happier if they can smile, laugh, and be happy again, too."

Joey went to sleep. When he awoke in the morning, he rushed into the kitchen to tell his Mom and Dad that he had seen and spoken to Kyle. Mom told him that it was only a dream.

"No, it wasn't," Joey insisted. He took his Mom by the hand. "Come, I'll show you where he was."

His Mom and Dad followed. When they got to the window they noticed something strange.

On the windowsill, there seemed to be handprints that sparkled. They looked out the window and saw footprints on the porch floor that also sparkled.

"Kyle was a shooting star," Joey told his parents. "He came to bring us a message. He said to tell you not to be sad anymore because he's all right. He wants us to laugh and smile and be happy again. You believe me, don't you?"

Both Mom and Dad kept looking at the handprints and footprints made of stardust and just nodded yes.